D0603460

Discarded by
Santa Maria Library

THE RACE OF THE CENTURY

Retold ~~Written~~ & illustrated by Barry Downard

SIMON & SCHUSTER BOOKS FOR YOUNG READERS
New York London Toronto Sydney

SIMON & SCHUSTER BOOKS FOR YOUNG READERS
An imprint of Simon & Schuster Children's Publishing Division
1230 Avenue of the Americas, New York, New York 10020

Design and art direction by Barry Downard.
The text for this book is set in Cromwell.
The illustrations for this book are the result of a lot of time spent taking photographs, snaffling them up in a photo-snaffling machine, and then sticking it all together with computer glue. No animals were hurt in the making of these images; in fact, they all had a real good time—B. D.
Manufactured in Mexico
1 2 3 4 5 6 7 8 9 10
Library of Congress Cataloging-in-Publication Data
Downard, Barry.
The race of the century/retold, written, and illustrated by Barry Downard—1st ed.
p. cm.
Summary: Fed up with his incessant taunting, Tom Tortoise challenges Flash Harry Hare to the race of the century, which turns into a worldwide media event, complete with television and newspaper coverage, photographers, and many other distractions.
ISBN-13: 978-1-4169-2509-5 (hardcover : alk. paper)
ISBN-10: 1-4169-2509-0 (hardcover : alk. paper)
1. Fables. 2. Animals—Fiction. 3. Humorous stories. I. Title.
PZ8.2.D68Fl 2008
398.24' 5—dc22
[E]
2006028791

Hi, kids!
Tortoises need very special diets, so please don't just pick them up and take them home. Besides, they might be in the middle of an important race!

Dedicated to the five women in my life:

Rosemary

Famous Tess

Cola Bear Butterbum

Fluff

Pixie

And my boy...

Mojo Mullet-Growlie

GASP!!

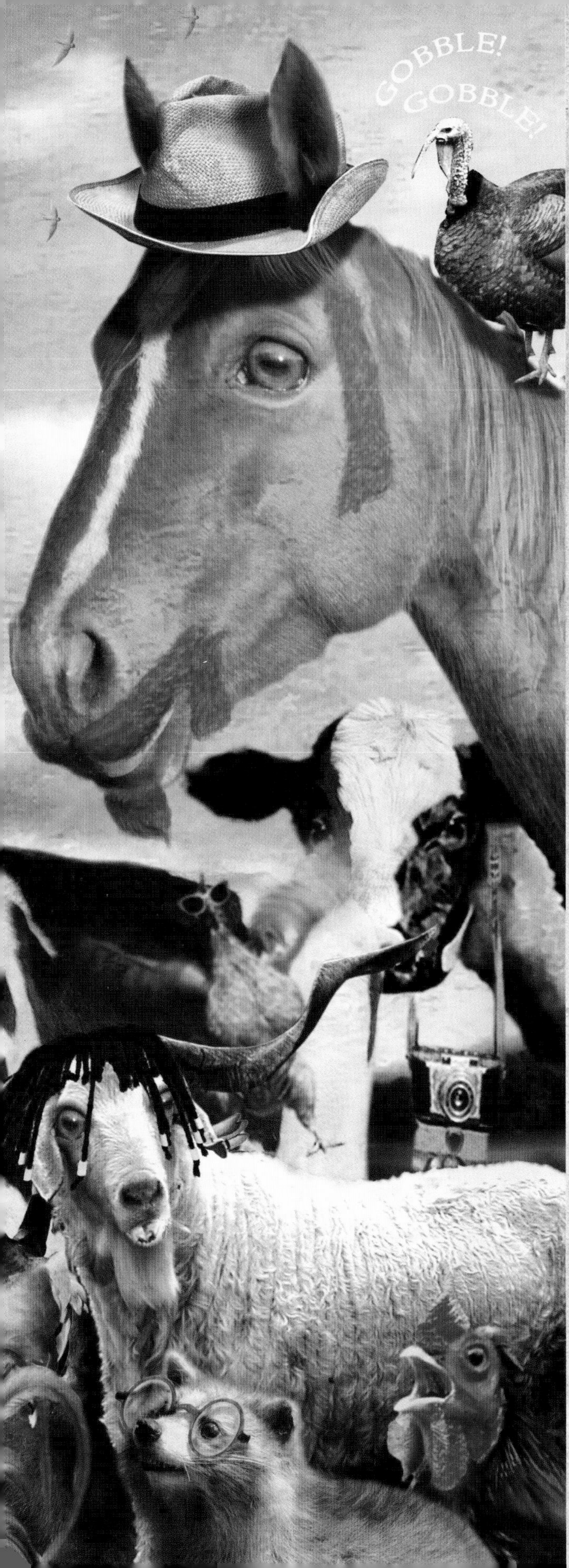

The residents of Critterville had *never* seen anything like it.

Ever!

After all his taunting
and boasting,
calling Tom Tortoise
"Twinkle Toes"
was the last straw.

Flash Harry Hare had
been challenged to a *race*
by Tom Tortoise!

Would you believe it?

The idea was so
hare-brained!

No Squawk Too Loud!
THE CRITTERVILLE CROON
HARE
VS
TORTOISE
"RACE OF THE CENTURY"

While everyone cackled and squawked, Tom Tortoise and Flash Harry Hare both started training for the big event . . . each in his own way.

JIM'S GYM
home
of
champiums

The big day finally arrived, and what an occasion it was.

The "Race of the Century" was on every beak, muzzle, and snout, as well as in every newspaper and magazine.

GOSH!
Critterville

It was even on TV!
HEE HAW HI! I'M DONKEY.
WELCOME TO CRITTER NEWS NETWORK
AND DONKEY'S WIDE WORLD OF SPORT!
TODAY WE PRESENT A LIVE BROADCAST
OF THE "RACE OF THE CENTURY"...
BETWEEN FLASH HARRY HARE
AND CHALLENGER, TOM TORTOISE!

OF SPORT
PONY

AND AS WE LINE UP FOR THE START OF THE RACE, WE WELCOME VIEWERS FROM AROUND THE WORLD!

"ON YOUR MARKS . . .

GET SET . . .

GO!"

The starter waved the flag, and off they went.

"See ya later, Twinkle Toes!" yelled Flash Harry Hare as he set off at top speed.

"Hmmmmph!" muttered Tom Tortoise.

"Cough, cough!" spluttered everyone else.

Flash Harry Hare sped off into the distance, leaving Tom Tortoise in his tracks.

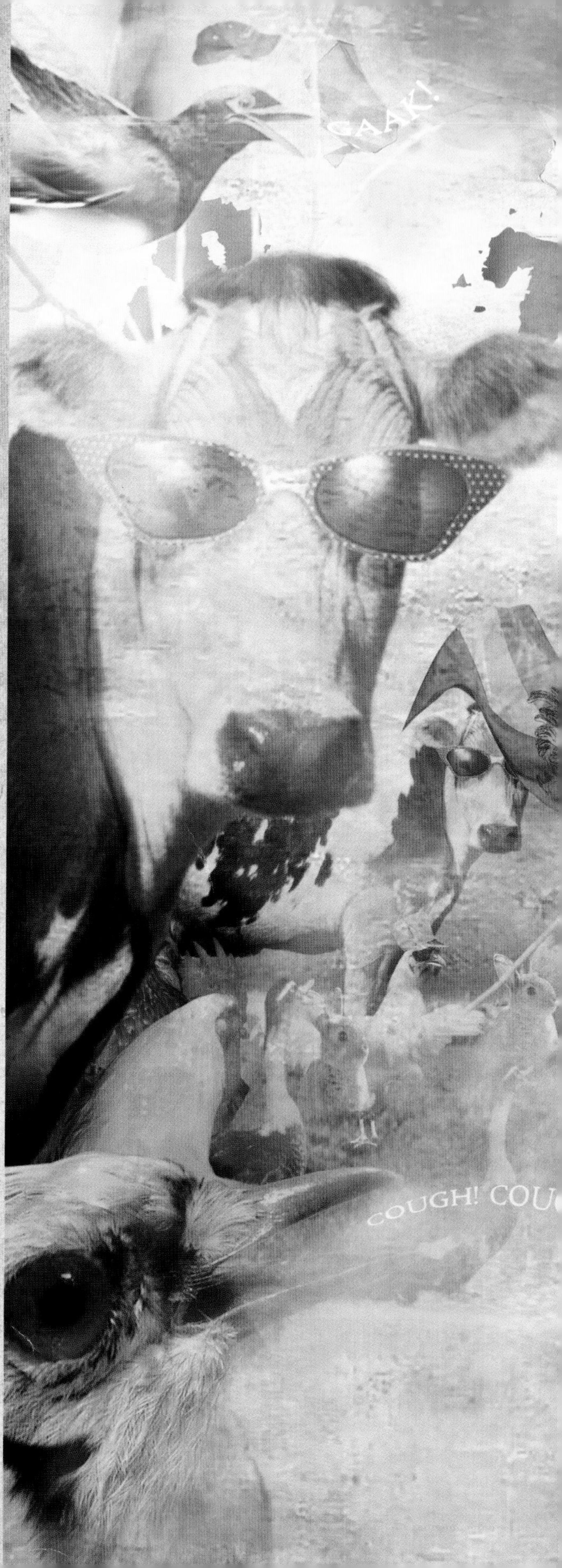

A R T
OBBLE!
GOBBLE!
COUGH! COUGH!

Flash Harry Hare
Flash Harry
CRITTERVILLE'S GREATEST

This is soooo easy,
thought Flash Harry Hare,
and soon he got sidetracked,
signing autographs for
fans . . .

. . . posing for photographs . . .
. . . posing for photographs . . .
and, err . . . oh, all right,
just one more . . .
. . . posing for photographs . . .

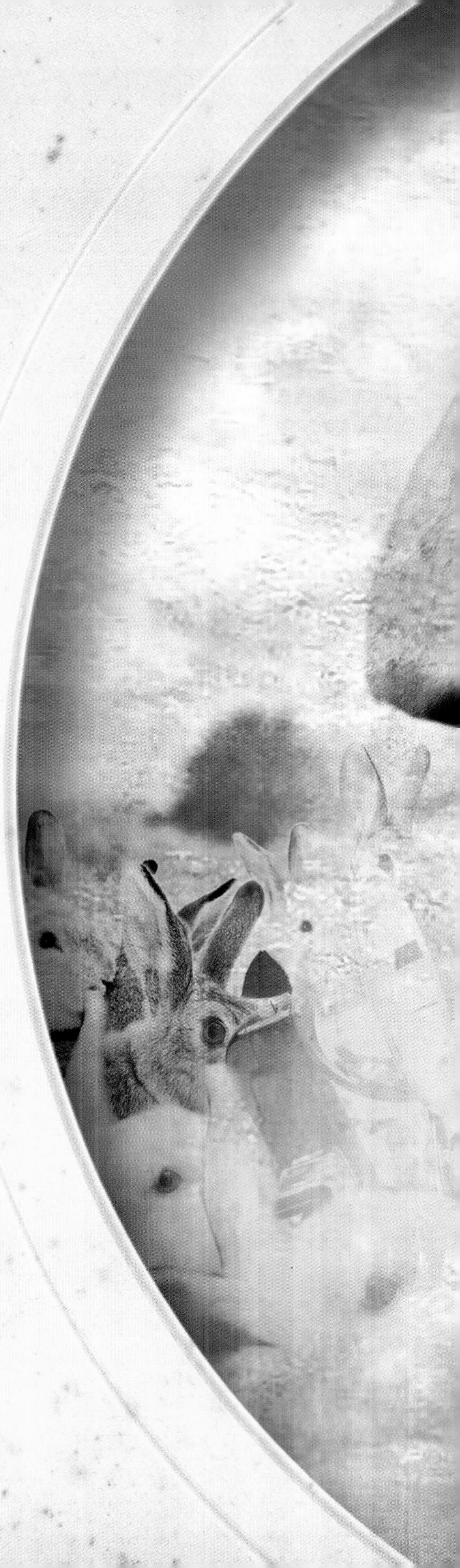

Bunnies Dig Me

. . . and getting a nibble to eat.

He started to get a little
bit drowsy.

*I'm so far ahead, and
Twinkle Toes is so slow that
my clothes are going out of
fashion. . . . I think I'll take
a nap,* he thought.

Fla Harry Hare

As Flash Harry Hare nodded off, Tom Tortoise plodded slowly but steadily on . . .

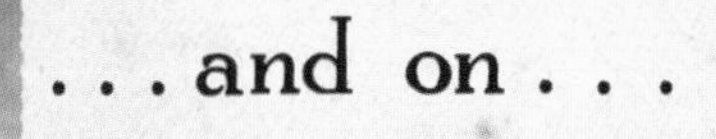

HEE HAW HI! JUST LOOK AT TOM GO!
THIS IS WORTH ANOTHER LOOK, FOR SURE!
WOW! THAT'S POETRY IN MOTION!

DON KEY'S
WIDE WORLD OF SPORT
GO!
SLOW - MO ACTION REPLAY
TORTOISE CAM
TELEBUNNIKIN

. . . right past a snoozing
Flash Harry Hare!

Hmmmmph!
thought Tom Tortoise.

Flash Harry Hare
FINISH

Snoozing Flash Harry Hare
woke with a start,
at the exact same moment
Tom Tortoise was about to
finish!

Everyone went wild!

YIPPEEE!!!

So, there's a lesson that Tom Tortoise taught us...

"Fast and flashy" doesn't always beat "slow and steady."

FLASH HARRY
HARE
HAS
BAD HARE DAY!
"RACE OF THE CENTURY"